This **TWO HOOTS** book belongs to

Frankie

For my sister Tiff, the true tiger in my life.

– A. P.

For all my nieces and nephews.

– S. M.

First published 2022 by Two Hoots
an imprint of Pan Macmillan
The Smithson, 6 Briset Street, London EC1M 5NR
EU representative: Macmillan Publishers Ireland Limited,
1st Floor, The Liffey Trust Centre, 117-126 Sheriff Street Upper
Dublin 1, D01 YC43
Associated companies throughout the world
www.panmacmillan.com
ISBN: 978-1-0350-2395-0
Text copyright © Alexandra Page 2022
Illustrations copyright © Stef Murphy 2022
Moral rights asserted.

1 3 5 7 9 8 6 4 2

A CIP catalogue record for this book is available from the British Library.
Printed in China
The illustrations in this book were made using mixed media and edited digitally in Photoshop.
Extra tiger drawing by Becka Evans, age 5.

www.twohootsbooks.com

ALEXANDRA PAGE

STEF MURPHY

The WORRY TIGER

TWO HOOTS

Long after bedtime, Rory was wide awake.
It was his turn for show-and-tell at school
the next day, but he wasn't ready.
What could he share that was special?

His thoughts felt as tangly
as tree roots.
His worries roared like the rain.
Rory wanted to hide.

Rory curled up inside his den, but his worries followed him.

Strange sounds began to hum and thrum.

Shadows rippled over the walls.

The air felt sticky and hot.

Rory looked out . . .

a jungle was growing!

Ferns unfurled from the floor.
Creepers clambered up the curtains.
Trees towered to the night sky.

Suddenly, Rory heard a drum-deep purr . . .

and a mighty tiger padded out of the den.

Rory wanted to run, until he heard her say in a friendly voice,

"Hello, Rory. I am your worry tiger."

Rory came closer and
reached up nervously.
The tiger's whiskers felt ticklish.
"Where are we?" Rory asked.

"Come with me," said the tiger, "and I'll show you around.
There are lots of things to see and many wonders to be found."

The jungle was a jumble of strange shapes and sounds and smells. But the tiger made almost no sound at all as she sauntered through the trees.

"Try this," said the tiger. "See how quiet you can be. Tiptoe like a tiger and tell me what you see."

Rory crept quietly.

He felt soft, squelchy earth
and damp leaves curling
between his toes.

Suddenly he saw . . .

"Fireflies!" Rory gasped.

As they followed the twinkling lights, the jungle
buzzed, clicked, whirred and whooped around them.

"Close your eyes," said the tiger, "and focus far and near.
Listen like a tiger and tell me what you hear."

Rory concentrated. "I hear crickets," he said.
"Frogs croaking in the trees. And . . .

"Monkeys!" laughed Rory.

They swooped and swung through the jungle.

"Stretch!" called the tiger. "Lift your arms up high.

Clamber like a tiger, until you see the sky."

Rory reached up into the branches.
He climbed higher and higher with
the worry tiger by his side, until . . .

they broke through the treetops.

"We're so high up," Rory said.

"Breathe in," said the tiger. "Let your tummy swell,
Then breathe out like a tiger and tell me what you smell."

Rory inhaled the sweet night air.

"Fruit and flowers," he said.

"And I think I smell rain!"

"Then we'd better hurry," said the tiger.

"It will soon be wet again!"

Rory and the tiger raced back
to the den, while raindrops
pitter-pattered all
around them.

"Will you still be here tomorrow, Tiger?"
Rory asked sleepily.

But the worry tiger had already curled

up and closed her eyes.

Rory snuggled into her soft warmth.

When Rory woke up his den
was stripy with sunlight.
"Tiger?" he called.
But she wasn't there.

School started soon and Rory still
had nothing special to share.

Then he had an idea.

When Rory's turn came for show-and-tell, his thoughts began to tangle
and his worries began to roar. But he remembered what the tiger had taught him.
He took a long, deep breath and showed the picture he had made.

"This is my worry tiger!" he said.

"She helped me to feel calm."

"That's very special, Rory," said his teacher.

"Would you like to tell us more?"

And he did.

Being mindful of ourselves and the world around us can help us to feel calm. Here are some things to try.

Tiptoe like a tiger

Move slowly across the floor, being as quiet as you can, like a tiger prowling through the jungle. Try to describe what you can see and feel.

Listen like a tiger

Sit or lie down somewhere comfy and close your eyes. Listen to the world around you. Name the different sounds you can hear.

Stretch like a tiger

Stretch your arms as wide as they can go. Reach up towards the sky as if you are touching the treetops. Try to imagine what you might find up there.

Breathe like a tiger

Sitting or lying down, take big tiger breaths in through your nose and out again through your mouth. You could put a favourite soft toy on top of your tummy and watch it rise and fall.

Make a tiger

Drawing, painting and being creative are good ways to feel calm. Try making a picture of a tiger, or another animal you like.